Hello, Family Members,

Learning to read is one of the most important accomplishments of early childhood. **Hello Reader!** books are designed to help children become skilled readers who like to read. Beginning readers learn to read by remembering frequently used words like "the," "is," and "and"; by using phonics skills to decode new words; and by interpreting picture and text clues. These books provide both the stories children enjoy and the structure they need to read fluently and independently. Here are suggestions for helping your child *before*, *during*, and *after* reading:

Before
- Look at the cover and pictures and have your child predict what the story is about.
- Read the story to your child.
- Encourage your child to chime in with familiar words and phrases.
- Echo read with your child by reading a line first and having your child read it after you do.

During
- Have your child think about a word he or she does not recognize right away. Provide hints such as "Let's see if we know the sounds" and "Have we read other words like this one?"
- Encourage your child to use phonics skills to sound out new words.
- Provide the word for your child when more assistance is needed so that he or she does not struggle and the experience of reading with you is a positive one.
- Encourage your child to have fun by reading with a lot of expression . . . like an actor!

After
- Have your child keep lists of interesting and favorite words.
- Encourage your child to read the books over and over again. Have him or her read to brothers, sisters, grandparents, and even teddy bears. Repeated readings develop confidence in young readers.
- Talk about the stories. Ask and answer questions. Share ideas about the funniest and most interesting characters and events in the stories.

I do hope that you and your child enjoy this book.

—Francie Alexander
Reading Specialist,
Scholastic's Learning Ventures

D0249650

For Samantha Marie Holmes,
who is always good to her grandfather!
—S.S. & J.B.

Copyright © 2001 by Susan Schade and Jon Buller.
All rights reserved. Published by Scholastic Inc.
SCHOLASTIC, HELLO READER, CARTWHEEL BOOKS and
associated logos are trademarks and/or registered trademarks of Scholastic Inc.

Library of Congress Cataloging-in-Publication Data

Schade, Susan.
    Space Dog Jack / by Susan Schade and Jon Buller.
        p.   cm. — (Hello reader! Level 1)
    Summary: A dog from Planet Woo sees all kinds of sights before visiting Earth and meeting Earth Dog Bob.
    ISBN 0-439-20541-7
    [1. Dogs — Fiction. 2. Life on other planets — Fiction. 3. Stories in rhyme.] I. Buller, Jon, 1943- II. Title. III. Series.
PZ8.3.S287   Sp 2000
[E] — dc21   00-023189

12 11 10 9 8 7 6 5 4 3 2 1   01 02 03 04 05

Printed in the U.S.A. 24
First printing, May 2001

SPACE DOG JACK

by Susan Schade & Jon Buller

Hello Reader! — Level 1

SCHOLASTIC INC.
Cartwheel BOOKS®

New York   Toronto   London   Auckland   Sydney
Mexico City   New Delhi   Hong Kong

I'm Space Dog Jack
of Planet Woo.
I live at number 22.

I go to school.
It is not far.
I drive my mini
space-jet car.

I like my teacher
and my friends.
I like it when
the school day ends.

In our garage,
for longer trips,
I keep my father's
old spaceships.

I like to blast off
and explore
where dogs have never
been before.

Inside the ship,
I float around.

I wear my helmet
on the ground.

It is no fun
on Planet Foo.
There isn't much
to see or do.

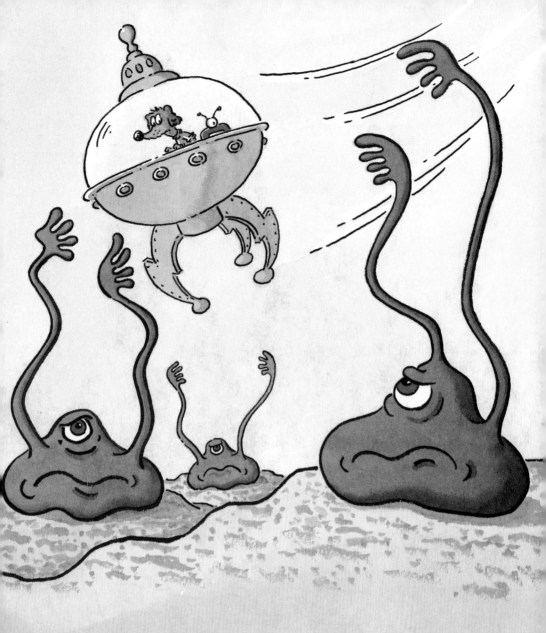

It is not safe
on Planet Yee.
The Yee Blobs try
to capture me!

There is no life
on Planet Zee.

At least, no life that I could see.

The warning button
flashes red—
strange planet looming
dead ahead!

The engine fails!
Prepare to crash!
I hit with a
GIGANTIC SPLASH!

I like these plants.
I like this smell.
It is a smell
I know quite well.

It is a dog!
"How do you do?
I'm Space Dog Jack.
What dog are you?"

It's Earth Dog Bob.
We sniff. We run.

I see the beach,
the surf, the sun.

Bob knows a girl
who has some glue,
some wire, and
a screw or two.

I stop the leak.

I mend the crack.

I say good-bye.

But I'll be back!